LOOK FOR IGGY'S OTHER TRIUMPHS

The Best of Iggy

IGGY

IS
BETTER
THAN
EVER

ILLUSTRATED BY SAM RICKS

G. P. Putnam's Sons

G. P. PUTNAM'S SONS
An imprint of Penguin Random House LLC, New York

Text copyright © 2020 by Annie Barrows
Illustrations copyright © 2020 by Sam Ricks

G. P. Putnam's Sons is a registered trademark of Penguin Random House LLC.

Visit us online at penguinrandomhouse.com

Library of Congress Cataloging-in-Publication Data
Names: Barrows, Annie, author. | Ricks, Sam, illustrator.
Title: Iggy is better than ever / Annie Barrows; illustrated by Sam Ricks.
Description: New York: G. P. Putnam's Sons, [2020] | Series: Iggy; [2] |
Summary: Fourth grader Iggy Frangi and his friends, afraid the principal
saw them pulling a big prank, vow to be so good they are invisible,
but learn that being too good causes trouble too.
Identifiers: LCCN 2020002311 (print) | LCCN 2020002312 (ebook) |
ISBN 9781984813336 | ISBN 9781984813343 (ebook)
Subjects: CYAC: Behavior—Fiction. | Schools—Fiction. | Friendship—Fiction.
Classification: LCC PZ7.B27576 Igg 2020 (print) | LCC PZ7.B27576 (ebook) |
DDC [Fic]—dc23
LC record available at https://lccn.loc.gov/2020002311
LC ebook record available at https://lccn.loc.gov/2020002312

Printed in the United States of America
ISBN 9781984813336

1 3 5 7 9 10 8 6 4 2

Design by Marikka Tamura
Text set in New Century Schoolbook LT Std.

For the real Miss Hackerman,
with sincere apologies
—A.B.

For Ruby Hill: wrecker of bicycles,
purveyor of fond memories
—S.R.

CONTENTS

CHAPTER 1

WHAT THIS BOOK ISN'T ABOUT

You know those books where the main kid becomes a better person at the end? You should. You've read about a million of them.

For example, the main kid excludes another kid, and then the other kid wins some big thing like a race and becomes really popular, and then the main kid feels left out, and from this, he learns to be nice and not to exclude anyone ever again. The end.

Sometimes, the main kid is already okay at

the beginning of the book, but he gets even better by the end. Say, the main kid *kills* at basketball, but by the end of the book, he learns that people who play the flute are just as good as people who kill at basketball. The end.

The main kid can also learn a rule, like Don't Light Stuff on Fire. Or he can learn to keep on trying even when the going gets tough. It can be anything. The point is for the main kid to be better at the end than he was at the beginning.

Would you like to know why there are so many books about becoming a better person?

Because grown-ups like it when kids get better. They think it's nice.

And they're right. It *is* nice.

Unfortunately, in this book, nobody gets any better.

Sorry.

Nobody gets any worse, though!

So that's good.

Iggy (that's the main kid, also known as the *hero*, of this book) stays pretty much the same all the way through. He learns a few things, but they aren't things that make him better. They are things about gardening supplies.

But mostly, Iggy gets in trouble. He does Thing 1, and then Thing 2 happens, and then, unfortunately, Thing 3 happens too. Does he learn from the bad things he does? Does he say to himself, Whew, that was really bad. I have learned my lesson. I'm going to stop doing that bad thing and become a better person!

No. He doesn't.

Some people think that kids will learn their lesson if they experience a terrible consequence when they do something wrong. For example, if you're not supposed to climb on the roof, but you do it anyway and then fall off and break your leg, this will teach you never to climb on the roof again. This is the whole idea behind punishments.

3

Punishments were invented for the times when you climb on the roof, but you don't end up with a broken leg. Grown-ups worry that you won't learn your lesson if there's no terrible consequence, so they make one up. That's what a punishment is.

Does Iggy get punished for doing his bad things?

He sure does!

Do his punishments make him wish he hadn't done them?

Not exactly.

To tell the truth, Iggy would do them all over again in a second.

Now, you are probably feeling kind of bad yourself because you're reading a book about a kid who doesn't get better. You're probably saying to yourself, Gosh, I wish I were reading a book about a kid who plants flowers by the side of the road instead of this book about Iggy getting in a bunch of trouble! If that's how you're feeling, I have some good news for you. Even though Iggy doesn't get any better during this book, *you* will. By reading about the bad things Iggy does, you will learn

4

not to do those things, and that will make you a better person. Isn't that great?

To help you become a better person, I am going to include special notes after each bad thing Iggy does to remind you that (a) boy, was that bad! and (b) don't do that! I'll even put the notes in big type so you can show them to your grown-up and say, "Look! Reading this book is making me a better person!" The big type will also make it easy for you to skip those parts if you don't want to read them.

But enough about you! Let's get to the bad things Iggy does. Like most bad things, it began on a . . .

CHAPTER 2

MONDAY

Here's Iggy on Monday morning. Yup, that's him.
That's his bowl of cereal. That's his dad. That's
his big sister, Maribel. His little sister is still
asleep.

Why is his head on the table?

Don't you ever put your head on the table?

No?

Well, aren't you polite.

Iggy looks like he's asleep, but he's not. He's thinking. He's thinking about how much he doesn't want to go to school.

"Eat your breakfast, Ig," says his dad.

"I don't want to go to school," Iggy says. Actually, he yells it.

But does anyone pay attention? No.

Maribel says, "I need a new backpack."

His mom, who isn't in this picture because she's in the next room looking at her computer, says something about how terrible the traffic is.

Then his dad says something else about how terrible the traffic is.

(Have you ever noticed how much time grown-ups spend talking about traffic?)

Iggy moans a little.

Does anyone feel sorry for him? No.

"We all have problems, Ig. Stop moaning and eat your breakfast," says his dad.

Guess what! You can eat breakfast and moan at the same time!

"Stop that. You like school," says Iggy's dad. "Remember last week you said Ms. Schulberger was your favorite teacher ever."

This is totally unfair. Ms. Schulberger *is* Iggy's favorite teacher ever, but liking your teacher isn't the same as liking school. He would probably like Ms. Schulberger even more if he only saw her once a month. Plus, he's only had four other teachers, so how can he know for sure she's his favorite? Maybe next year, in fifth grade, he'll have a teacher he likes better than Ms. Schulberger. He says this.

"Ha," says Maribel. She's eleven, so she's in middle school, but she used to go to Iggy's school. "You'll have either Ms. Keets or Miss Hackerman, and you better hope you get Miss Hackerman, because Ms. Keets will kill you."

Iggy frowns. Why would she kill him?

Maribel leans over her cereal and whispers, "In my year, there was this kid who fell out of his chair by mistake, and Ms. Keets cut his hat."

"Whaddaya mean, cut his hat?" whispers Iggy.

"In the paper cutter," says Maribel. "He fell out of his chair by *mistake*. So think what Ms. Keets would do to you."

Iggy thinks. He thinks about all the times he's fallen out of his chair on purpose. Sometimes he yells "Whooo!" when he does it. Sometimes he pretends to trip when he's going to the whiteboard. Sometimes—hardly ever—he slides under the table and ties other kids' shoelaces together so they fall over when they stand up.

10

Ms. Keets probably *would* kill him.

"What about Miss Hackerman?" Hackerman! It sounds like she would kill him too.

Maribel shrugs. "Miss Hackerman's nice. She wouldn't kill you, because she likes everyone. But she's old. She could be gone by next year. She was sick for something like a month when I had her. And guess who our substitute was."

"Who?"

"Mrs. Wander." Maribel grins at Iggy and makes a chopping motion across her throat. "*Ha-ack!*" she chokes.

Is Maribel choking on her cereal? No. She isn't. What is she doing, then? And why?

Let me explain . . .

CHAPTER 3

A SHORT CHAPTER ABOUT A SHORT PERSON

Mrs. Wander is the principal at Iggy's school. She is very short. She's so short that most fifth graders and even some fourth graders are taller than she is. There's nothing wrong with being short. Plenty of people are short and funny. Plenty of people are short and friendly. But Mrs. Wander is not these things.

Mrs. Wander is short and scary.

When kids see Mrs. Wander coming, they stand completely still, hoping her eyes will slide over them. Mrs. Wander doesn't like kids who move. She especially doesn't like kids who run.

13

Running, she says, is not safe. Mrs. Wander is crazy about safety. She loves it. In Iggy's opinion, it isn't very safe to be so scary that you almost make kids pass out when they see you. But nobody's asked Iggy's opinion.

Here's another thing about Mrs. Wander: She doesn't like Iggy very much.

Actually, she doesn't seem to like him at all.

They have spent a lot of time together, especially the year Iggy was in second grade. That year, he was sent to her office so many times, he had his own chair. Mrs. Wander even put a sign with his name on it on the chair. Iggy thought that was mean.

Sometimes people like you more when they get to know you. Not Mrs. Wander. The more she got to know Iggy, the less she liked him. When Mrs. Wander saw Iggy, her eyeballs would bulge

with fury, even if he was standing completely still (which, to be honest, he usually wasn't).

So what would happen if Mrs. Wander were his teacher?

Iggy would have to run away to Ketchum, Idaho.

CHAPTER 4

LATER,
YOU ASK YOURSELF
WHY

As it turned out, school wasn't as bad as Iggy had thought it was going to be, but still, the best part about it was that it ended.

After school, Iggy and Diego went to Arch's house. Iggy, Diego, and Arch had been friends since the second day of kindergarten, when they had made a racetrack out of carpet squares and tore around on it until Arch broke the white-board with his head. Kindergarten was fun! Now, in fourth grade, there were no carpet squares, no racetrack, and actually, no Diego, since after kindergarten, the school had made a rule that Diego and Iggy could never be in the same classroom again.

They could still hang out after school, though.

Arch had lots of good stuff in his house, including a million computer games and one of those vacuums that rolls around by itself and a wheelchair and the sports channel and this crazy hot room with birds in it. First they played *Invisitor* until Arch's guy was buried under a glacier and he quit; then they all got in the wheelchair and zipped around; then they tried to get the vacuum to bang into them (but it wouldn't); then they went into the crazy hot

bird room and meowed
like cats until the birds
freaked out; and then
Arch's mom made them
go outside.

They stood around in the front yard for a
while.

Then they stood around in the backyard for
a while.

"How much longer do we have to
stay out here?" asked Diego.

Meow!

MEOOWWW...

Mwoww

MEEOwww...

Arch said probably something like an hour.

An hour!

"Let's do something," said Iggy.

"Like what?" said Arch.

"Like something fun," said Iggy. He glanced around Arch's backyard. "What's in your shed?"

Arch shrugged. "I don't know. Gardening stuff, I guess."

"A leaf blower?" asked Diego.

A leaf blower! You can have tons of fun with a leaf blower!

They raced for the shed—but there was no leaf blower. There was no weed whacker either. There wasn't even a lawn mower. There were folding chairs and a Christmas tree holder and some shovels and bags of smelly dirt and a big roll of clear plastic tape.

"We could stack up the chairs," suggested Arch.

Iggy and Diego said that was stupid.

"We could bury the chairs," suggested Arch.

Iggy and Diego said that was stupid.

"We could bury each other," suggested Arch.

"Cool!" said Diego. He picked up a shovel. "Let's bury Iggy, since he's the shortest."

Iggy thought about being buried. Dirt piling up around him, and then over him, covering his hands, his mouth, his nose . . . "Wait!" he said. "I've got a better idea."

21

Arch and Diego looked at him a certain way. This certain way said that they didn't think he had a better idea, that he was a big chicken, and that they might bury him whether he wanted them to or not.

"Here!" said Iggy. He grabbed the big roll of clear plastic tape.[*] (This thing is an asterisk; it means you're supposed to look at the bottom of the page.) "This is going to be hecka funny! We'll stretch this across your street, Arch, and see what happens when cars drive through it."

"Dude. Nothing's going to happen," said Diego. "It'll just break."

"You don't know that," said Iggy. He yanked out a piece of tape and stretched it a little. "Maybe it'll be like a big rubber band and shoot them backward. You don't know."

"It's going to break," said Arch. "For sure."

"I swear we'll dig you up before you suffocate," said Diego.

----

*This is not regular, sticky tape. This is called gardening tape, or sometimes tie tape, and it's for tying plants to sticks to keep them from falling over. It's not sticky, but it's a little bit stretchy, so the plants can grow.

Dirt closing over his head! "I'll bet you a dollar it won't break," said Iggy. "A dollar each."

Diego and Arch looked at each other. "Okay," they said together.

CHAPTER 5

SOMETIMES, YOU HAVE MORE FUN THAN YOU EXPECT

Mostly, you don't have more fun than you expect. Mostly, you have either just about as much fun as you expect or less fun than you expect. But sometimes, especially when you don't expect much fun at all, you have a great time.

This is what happened to Iggy and Diego and Arch that afternoon.

They started by being lucky. When they got to the front yard, they saw that just up the block from Arch's house, there were two trees exactly opposite each other on either side of the street. One was between the sidewalk and the street and one was in a front yard, but the important thing was this: They were lined up. Iggy circled the tape around one tree trunk. Then he crossed the street, unwinding the tape as he went, and circled it around the opposite tree trunk. The tape was about three feet off the ground.

Arch and Diego watched him. "This is boring!" yelled Diego.

"Wait till a car comes!" yelled Iggy.

They didn't have to wait very long, because maybe half a minute later, a little blue car came down the street and drove right into Iggy's tape.

Did the tape shoot the car backward, hurling it through the air in the direction it had come?

Well, no, it didn't. But it didn't just snap either. Which, truthfully, was what Iggy had been expecting. Of course, the tape broke, but it

tree 1

accomplices

garden tape
(NOW WITH 10% MORE STRET

didn't break right away.
First it stretched for a couple
of seconds, and—this was the really
great part—there was a tiny moment when
the car was pushing against the tape, and the tape
was holding it back. And in that tiny moment,
the driver got an incredibly weird expression
on his face. It was sort of curiosity—what *was*
that?—and sort of fear—what was *that*?—and it
was completely hilarious.

The tape broke, and the car drove on, the
driver looking nervously right and left.

"SWEET!" shouted Diego, popping out from behind his tree. "Did you see his face?"

"He was freaking!" yelled Iggy.

"Let's do it again," Arch called, laughing.

So they did.

unsuspecting vehicle

tree 2

mastermind

The next time, they got an old lady in a black car. Even with all her windows rolled up, they could hear her yell "Gah!" which made it *so much* funnier. She drove away fast.

"This is great!" hollered Diego. "She totally thought it was aliens!"

The time after that, they got a guy in a truck. He stopped and rolled down his window and looked back toward the trees, but luckily, Iggy hid behind his tree, and Arch and Diego crouched down in some bushes.

As time went on, they learned that women usually drove away as fast as they could and men usually stopped, rolled down the window, and looked back at the road. But since the tape was clear, and Iggy, Arch, and Diego were hiding, they didn't see anything, and then they drove on.

You'd think it would get old, after eleven cars, but that's because you weren't there. It just got funnier and funnier and funnier.

Until the twelfth car.

CHAPTER 6

THE TWELFTH CAR

For the twelfth time, they tied the tape around the trees, Iggy on his side of the street, Diego and Arch on theirs. "We're going to run out of tape pretty soon!" Iggy yelled, waving the (much smaller) roll of tape.

"Let's make this one a double," Diego yelled back. "Since it's the last one."

Great idea! The boys quickly set up a second strand of tape across the street and ran back to their places.

"This is going to be the best!" Iggy yelled, because—as all three of them knew—two strands of tape meant that the next car would get twice the pushing-backward feeling. But it also meant—as none of them noticed—that the car would be slowed down twice as much. So if the first eleven cars broke through the tape in one to two seconds, the twelfth car would break through the tape in two to *four* seconds. Four seconds may not sound like very long—and it isn't—but it can *feel* very long.

Ah-one.

Ah-two.

Ah-three.

Ah-four.

See what I mean?

But, as I mentioned, none of them thought about that.

Iggy was already laughing when he saw the red car in the distance. "All right! Here it comes!" he hollered.

Diego and Arch pretended to be the car, boinging backward. They fell onto the ground near the bushes.

Which is why Iggy was the only one who saw

the face of the driver coming toward the double strand of tape. It was a very familiar face. It was a face that made him want to stand completely still.

Which, under the circumstances, was not a very good idea.

Because—yup, you guessed it!—the driver of the car was Mrs. Wander.

On she came, right
into the double strand
of tape, which held for one, two,
three—only it was more like ooonnnne, twoooooo,
threeeee—seconds before it broke.

And yes, Mrs. Wander got that same expression on her face that every other driver had—What *was* that? What was *that*?—before the tape broke.

And yes, Mrs. Wander looked nervously right and left.

But after that, Mrs. Wander was different, because she slammed on her brakes, pulled over to the side of the road, got out of her car, and began to stomp toward the broken pieces of tape.

RIP
IGGY FRANGI

WELL, HE
DIDN'T
GET WORSE.

Iggy's life passed
before his eyes.

Did he think: Stretching clear plastic tape across the road is very bad, and I deserve whatever punishment I get?

No. He didn't think that.

Did he think: I have now learned my lesson, and I will never do that bad thing again?

Nope. He didn't think that either.

Did he even think: I must warn my friends of approaching danger?

Nah.

He thought: GET OUT OF HERE! NOW! BEFORE I GET CAUGHT!!

And then he ran and ran and ran.

CHAPTER 7

THE WANDERING THOUGHTS OF IGGY AND ARCH

Late that night (okay, it was only 8:14), Iggy called Arch.

"She hasn't called my parents," said Arch.

"She hasn't called mine either," said Iggy.

"She didn't call Diego's either," said Arch. "I think she didn't see us."

"How could she not see us?" asked Iggy. "We were running all over the place."

"I don't know," said Arch. "Maybe she was only looking at the tape."

"No," said Iggy. "I know her better than you guys. I think she's waiting until school to-morrow, and then she's going to call us in and scream at us and tell our parents. And then probably she's going to call the police."

"She's not going to call the police," said Arch (but he sounded worried).

"You don't know her like I do," said Iggy.

"Why wouldn't she call them tonight, if she was going to call them?" asked Arch.

"So we'll freak out about it all night," said Iggy. "That's why."

"No," said Arch (but he still sounded worried). "I think she's not sure. I think she wasn't really looking around because she was so mad, and she's not sure it was us."

"Maybe," said Iggy. It was possible. "Maybe she only saw us a little."

"Yeah," said Arch. "Just for a split second. She's probably thinking: Who were those guys? I know I've seen them somewhere."

Iggy began to feel a tiny bit hopeful. "Maybe if she doesn't see us tomorrow, she won't figure it out."

"Yeah, okay. I'm going to be invisible tomorrow," said Arch. "I'm going to be a ninja."

"Same," said Iggy. "No one's even going to know I'm there. I'm going to be so quiet and good, Arden's going to look like a criminal next to me." Arden was a girl in their class who was always perfect. She was a pain.

Arch laughed. "Me too."

Iggy didn't feel very worried now. He would be completely invisible for a day, and Mrs. Wander wouldn't even think of him, much less remember seeing him at the scene of the crime. He thought about her face when she drove through the tape. "Do you think you're going to get some more of that tape?"

"I told my dad we needed more," said Arch.

"Invite me over when he gets it," said Iggy.

HOW TO BE A BETTER PERSON, PART ONE

Now, kids, I am sorry to say that Iggy didn't learn his lesson. But you did, right?

What did you learn?

You learned NEVER to tie clear plastic tape across a street! Never, never, never!

Is it fun?

Yes!

But is it also bad?

Yes!

And you will NEVER do it, right?

Right!

Whew! You have been saved from gardening-tape badness! You are so much better than you were before!

CHAPTER 8

IGGY
THE INVISIBLE

It is now time to discuss the peacock flounder.

The peacock flounder is a fish, not a peacock. It's called a peacock flounder because sometimes it appears to have bright blue-green spots on its sides. While this is probably a total blast for the peacock flounder, we don't care about blue spots. We care about the fact that the peacock flounder can change the color of its spots from gray to brown or white or blue-green or whatever color will help it blend into its background. The point—for the peacock flounder—is to become invisible so its predators don't eat it.*

The next day at school, Iggy was a peacock flounder.

---

*Good work! You are really getting the hang of the asterisk thing. Do you want to know something else completely cool about the peacock flounder? Its eyeballs are on the ends of little stumps that turn in different directions so that one eye can look forward and one can look backward at the same time.

He blended in with all the good children who would *never, ever* tie plastic tape across a street and then laugh at the people who drove through it.

Iggy sat quietly at his desk with his hands folded. He didn't run. He didn't yell. He didn't tap the gecko tank. He didn't see if he could land a three-point shot with his napkin from the lunch table to the garbage can. He didn't make fun of Arden during PE. He didn't laugh when Owen's shoes got ruined during science.

All day long, he was a peacock flounder. All day long, he was waiting to hear the intercom buzz and then the school secretary's voice: "Ms. Schulberger, please send Iggy Frangi to the principal's office."

But it never happened. She didn't call in Arch or Diego either.

"I think we're okay," said Diego at the end of school. But he looked over his shoulder as he said it.

"Yeah," said Arch. "I think she didn't see us."

Iggy thought about Mrs. Wander's bulging eyeballs. "I'm going to be good for one more day," he said. "Just to be sure."

So the next day, Iggy remained invisible to his predators. He sat quietly at his desk with his hands folded.

"Are you feeling okay, Iggy?" asked Ms. Schulberger.

Iggy nodded. He nodded with his mouth shut because he was afraid he'd yell if he opened it.

Actually, he wasn't feeling okay. He was feeling like his eyes were going to pop out of his head. Is this how good kids felt all the time? How could anyone sit still for this long? He was going to explode. By noon, he was making little exploding sounds in his throat.

He tried to be quiet and well-behaved. He really did.

He only threw his napkin a little way across the lunchroom. He waited calmly by the sports equipment shed to get a basketball. He waited so calmly that all the basketball courts were taken by the time he got to the blacktop and none of the fifth graders would let him in, when he was just as good as most of them and better than four of them (and you know who I'm talking about here, Marc, Jadyn, Chris, and Kelsey). Still, Iggy waited patiently for them to finish, just standing there at the farthest edge of the blacktop with his basketball.

Just standing there, waiting . . .

CHAPTER 9

GOOD THINGS COME TO THOSE WHO WAIT. BUT THEN AGAIN, SO DO BAD THINGS

I have to say something about Miss Hackerman. Some people might call it rude, but if they did, they'd be wrong. It's just true.

Miss Hackerman is old. Very old. Miss Hackerman is so old that sometimes her students' parents had also been her students, and at Open House, they stand around talking about how great life was in 1985. Miss Hackerman is so old that she wears slippers when she's in her classroom. When she has to leave the classroom, she sits down in a chair and puts on real-people shoes, and she makes faces when she wears them, like *ouch, ouch, ouch*. Miss Hackerman is so old that she calls the kids in her class "boys and girls." When it is time to line up to go back to class after lunch recess, she calls in a quavering voice, "Come along, boys and girls! Lunch is over, boys and girls!"

Ms. Schulberger calls, "Room 20! People! Time to come in!"

When the kids hear their teachers call them in, everyone who has a ball groans and tries to get in one last final throw or kick before his or her teacher blows the whistle. The whistle means: You are going to be in trouble in about ten seconds.

Iggy was still waiting patiently when the teachers started coming out of their secret lunchroom. Nah, he thought. Recess isn't over. It can't be over yet. They must be early.

He hadn't even shot his basketball *once*.

The teachers strolled to their line-up spots in various places around the blacktop.

They've got to be early, thought Iggy. He began to feel less patient. "Come on, you guys," he said to the fifth graders. "Let me come in, just for a minute. Recess is almost over."

Marc said a thing that meant No. Chris laughed.

That was mean.

(Some people could really use a book on how to become a better person.)

"Room 20! Time to come in, people!" called Ms. Schulberger.

"Nooo!" groaned Iggy. He had waited all recess long! What a waste of a basketball!

"Children!" quavered Miss Hackerman. "Boys and girls!"

Hooray! The fifth graders had to go in! That meant there might be a couple of seconds for Iggy to throw an outside shot.

Marc took one last shot. Jadyn took one last shot.

Hurry up! thought Iggy. "Come on, you guys!" he yelled.

"Iggy!" called Ms Schulberger. "Hop to it!" She blew her whistle.

Kelsey gave Iggy a look—a you-just-missed-your-entire-recess-you-loser look—and took one last shot.

Stupid fifth graders! They acted like they owned the world. Iggy hated them. Angrily, he

turned and started to run toward Ms. Schulberger's line, dribbling the ball—*whap, whap*—as he went. Remember how I said Iggy had been waiting at the farthest edge of the blacktop? He had a long way to run. All the other courts were empty now. All the other hoops were now perfectly free.

Including the one that was closest to the fifth-grade lines.

I'll show those losers who can throw a ball, thought Iggy. I'll show them.

Whap, whap, whap—

"Iggy!" called Ms. Schulberger, not patiently. "Now!"

Dang! Iggy jumped into the air and hurled the ball as hard as he could toward the basketball hoop next to the fifth graders.

What a throw.

What a beautiful, long, perfect throw.

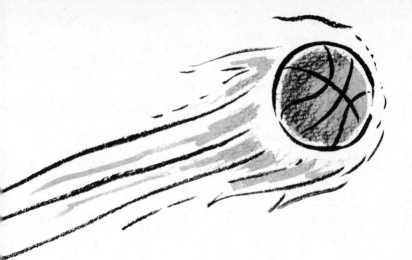

If he had made the basket, it would have been the greatest outside shot in basketball history. Every kid in his school would have remembered it forever.

But Iggy didn't make the basket. He missed the basket.

In fact, he not only missed the basket, he actually missed the entire court. The ball sailed at top speed over the backboard, through the air, and right to the front of the fifth-grade line, where it slammed right into Miss Hackerman's shoulder.

Miss Hackerman's head boinged from side to side.

And then Miss Hackerman crumpled to the ground like a sack of potatoes.

And then every kid in school—all nicely lined up on the blacktop—turned and pointed to Iggy and screamed, "Iggy killed Miss Hackerman!"

CHAPTER 10

DEATH
AND
BASKETBALLS

Obviously, Iggy did *not* kill Miss Hackerman.

Duh.

Of course not.

Number 1: As you know, this is a kids' book. And Iggy is the main character, otherwise known as the *hero* of the book. The hero of a kids' book is not going to kill anyone, especially not a teacher. If I wrote a book in which Iggy had actually killed Miss Hackerman with a basketball, do you know what would happen to me? Author jail, that's what.

But also, Number 2: You can't kill someone with a basketball. It's just not possible.

What?

Even if the person is really old and weak?

Hm.

Let me go ask Steph Curry.

. . .

. . .

. . .

Okay. Steph says he never heard of anyone being killed by a basketball. (He also says don't go throwing basketballs at people who aren't playing basketball.)

(Which Iggy wasn't. He was throwing the basketball at the basket and missed.)

• • •

Back to Miss Hackerman.*

Last time we saw her, Miss Hackerman was crumpled on the blacktop like a sack of potatoes. Poor Miss Hackerman.

But, as we have just discussed, she was not crumpled and dead. She was only crumpled.

Did she get a concussion?

No!

Iggy hit her on the shoulder, so Miss Hackerman crumpled sideways, and the first thing that hit the ground was not her head. It was her arm.

Did she break her arm?

No!

Did she break anything?

Yes. She broke her teacup.

Did she break any body parts?

No. She didn't.

I'm not saying she felt good. She didn't feel

---

*If you have read a book called *The Best of Iggy*, you may be saying to yourself, "Hey, didn't he hurt a teacher in that book too?" Yup, he did. He was sorry about that. You may be asking, "Does this kid hurt all his teachers?" No. His first-grade teacher got through the whole year without a scrape.

good. She was shaken up, and she got a really big bruise on her elbow and another one on her leg.

She was so shaken up that she had to take the rest of the day off. The school secretary had to teach her class.

None of that was good, and I'm not saying it was. Even if Iggy did not kill Miss Hacker-man, even if Iggy did not seriously injure Miss

Hackerman, it was very hard on poor, old Miss Hackerman, getting hit with a basketball and crumpling to the ground. I am *really sorry* that Iggy hit Miss Hackerman with that basketball. And so was he.

But the fact remains: Miss Hackerman was okay.

After a couple of days.

CHAPTER 10½

HOW TO BE A BETTER PERSON, PART TWO

Oh my gosh, kids! What have you learned from this terrible story?

You have learned that you must never, ever throw balls around on the playground! (What the heck else are you going to do with a ball, though?)

You mustn't throw a ball, because you might hit someone!

And that would be dangerous.

You should never, ever do anything dangerous.

Safety first!

Safety is the most important thing in the world!

So, kids, don't throw balls. Don't run. Don't talk with your mouth full.

Promise me you'll never, ever do any of these things!

Never, never, never!

Great! You are so safe now!

Plus, you are so much better than you were before you started reading this book.

CHAPTER 11

THERE ARE
SOME QUESTIONS
YOU SHOULDN'T
ANSWER

Way back before you were a better person, you learned that the school secretary taught Miss Hackerman's class after Iggy hit Miss Hackerman with the basketball. Guess why it was the school secretary, who wasn't even a real teacher, who taught the class, instead of Mrs. Wander.

That's right! You're so smart.

Because Mrs. Wander
was busy yelling at Iggy.
Actually, she wasn't yelling
the whole time. She talked, *blah-
blah-blah*, and then suddenly she yelled
when she got to words like "irresponsible"
and "dangerous" and "self-control" and
"lack of respect" and "rules" and
"if you can't" and "then we'll have to"
and "we cannot have this kind of"
and "you are lucky you didn't"
and, in the end, "Do you understand
what you've done
wrong, Iggy?"

(If this book were about
Iggy becoming a better person, this is the place it would
happen. He would think back
to the gardening tape and re-
alize that all his troubles had
started there. He would say to

80

himself, If I had never played that trick with the gardening tape, I wouldn't be in trouble now. I am going to stop playing tricks and start planting flowers by the side of the road. He would tell this to Mrs. Wander and add, "Thank you, Mrs. Wander, for teaching me how to be a better person." And then she would smile at him, because she was really nice underneath it all. And then they would dance or something.)

(However, this book is not about that.)

"Do you understand what you've done wrong, Iggy?" asked Mrs. Wander.

"Yes," said Iggy. He knew exactly what he had done wrong. He had tried to be quiet and good. He had tried to be good so Mrs. Wander wouldn't call him into her office and yell at him about gardening tape, and what happened? He had ended up in her office with her yelling at him about basketballs.

Obviously, he had tried too hard. If he had not waited patiently but had busted into the fifth graders' game, he wouldn't have been so mad at the end of recess. If he hadn't been so mad at the end of recess, he wouldn't have tried to make the long shot to the basket near the fifth-grade line. If he hadn't tried to make the long shot, the ball wouldn't have hit Miss Hackerman. And if he hadn't hit Miss Hackerman, she wouldn't have crumpled to the ground, and he wouldn't have lost all chance of getting her instead of Ms. Keets for his teacher next year. Now Miss Hackerman would never allow him in her class. He was going to be stuck with Ms. Keets. His life was ruined.

So, yes, Iggy had learned his lesson. He would never try to be that good again. Was he going to try to be bad? No. No, no, no! He didn't *want* to be bad. He wanted to be the way he was. And the way he was, it wasn't *bad*. He might *do* something bad, but *he* wasn't bad. BAD and IGGY were not equal. He didn't think so, anyway. So maybe he would try to stop doing this bad thing or that bad thing. But trying to be one hundred percent completely good? It just led to trouble.*

"Tell me what you've learned, Iggy," asked Mrs. Wander.

This is what's called a trick question.

Iggy knew he shouldn't tell Mrs. Wander what he had, in fact, learned. So this is what he said: "I learned I should go to basketball camp this summer. I mean, I know I'm going to get better when I'm taller, and it's not like anyone else could've made that basket—it was like three hundred feet, so no way—but still, I need to work on my outside shot. I wasn't aiming for Miss Hackerman," he added. "So could I please be in her class next year?"

For some reason, this answer caused Iggy to get suspended.

---

*By the way, this is a paragraph you should definitely not show to grown-ups. Even though it's true.

84

CHAPTER 12

DAD IS GRUMPY

I am sorry to say that Iggy had enough experience being suspended to hope that his mom would be the one to stay home with him the next day.

It was his dad.

His dad wasn't terrible or anything. Most of the time, his dad was A-OK. But sometimes his dad got grumpy, and Iggy getting suspended was one of the things that made him grumpy.

Iggy expected a certain amount of grumpiness when he got suspended. He expected that his parents were going to give him a talking-to and he was going to feel bad. He expected that he was going to have to write an apology. He expected that he was going to get "defunded," which is what his mom and dad called no allowance. He expected that he would get privileges revoked, which meant no video games for—ugh—two weeks. He expected that he would have to do some really gross chore, like washing the kitchen garbage can. He expected that he wouldn't be allowed to do anything fun during the suspended day.

But in addition to all that, Iggy's dad glared. The whole day, he glared at Iggy.

Iggy's mom wasn't like that. She did the things Iggy expected—talking-to, no fun, chores—but in the end, she always seemed more sorry than mad. And, unlike his dad, on a suspended day, she didn't want to waste her entire day off work being sorry or mad. By the afternoon, she and Iggy were usually watching a movie. Granted, it was usually some girls-in-long-dresses movie, but Iggy didn't mind, especially if his mom made hot chocolate. He never would have said it (because he wasn't stupid), but he liked being suspended if his mom stayed home with him.

This time, however, it was his dad. Glaring.

And not only glaring, but muttering.

He muttered things about "Some of us have a job, you know" and "If *I* get suspended, you'll be sorry" and "Irresponsible and immature."

Jeez. It wasn't like Iggy had *wanted* to be suspended.

Didn't his dad like having the day off?

No. Apparently, he didn't.

Iggy wondered what his dad really did. Because what he *said* he did sounded so incredibly boring that he should have been glad to have the day off. But he wasn't glad.

So he must have a secret job.

Maybe he was a spy!

Had to be.

Because about halfway through the day, Iggy's dad was so crazy about his job that he said, "I'm going to try to get some work done, and I don't want to hear a peep out of you.

Unless you're bleeding, don't bug me." He put his computer on the dining room table.

Iggy stood in the hall, not bugging anyone.

After a minute, his dad looked up, glaring. "Go outside. Go outside and—and— pick weeds. Or something. Don't bug me."

CHAPTER 13

OR SOMETHING

Iggy went outside and picked weeds. He really did. For ten minutes, he picked weeds. Then he picked up a big rock in his front yard and looked at all the slimy, wormy things under it. That was fun. He picked up three more rocks. Gross!

Then he looked at his street. So this was what it was like while he was in school.

Quiet. Empty. Amazingly empty.

No cars drove down the street.

No people walked along the sidewalk.

It was weird. Why were there no people?

Someone should be walking along the sidewalk, at least.

Iggy went down the front steps to the sidewalk and looked right. No one.

He looked left. No one.

Nothing.

Iggy lived on the most boring street in the world.

Is this what being a grown-up was going to be like?

Quiet and empty?

It was horrible!

Iggy felt like he had to *do* something, something fast and fun. He looked back at his house. "Don't bug me," his dad had said. "Go pick weeds—or something."

Or something. That's what he had said. So it would be okay if Iggy got on his skateboard and—

Except his skateboard was inside the house. Going inside to get the board might count as bugging Dad.

Also, Dad might tell him he had to stay in the yard.

Okay. He would do something fast and fun on his bike.

Iggy went to the spot next to the fence where his bike was kept and unlocked it. He was pretty quiet about this, because he didn't want to bug good old Dad.

He hadn't been on his bike in a while. It was fun! More fun than he remembered. First, he went super fast down the block and slammed on the brake at the corner. He thought he almost burned rubber. On the next block, he went faster and longer, and *then* he stood up when he slammed on the brake. Still, not quite.

On the next block, he mixed it up—wheelies. Fun.

He wished he had a ramp.

He turned down the next block.

Whoa! A ramp!

It wasn't a real ramp, of course. It was a big pile of dirt, but it wasn't really dirt; it was dirt and bark and stuff mixed together.[*] Iggy didn't know why anyone would have a big pile of dirt sitting on the sidewalk in front of their house, but he did know that people put things out on the sidewalk when they wanted other people to use them. His mom, for instance, put a bucket of lemons by the sidewalk when their lemon tree went nuts. She was glad when people took them.

Iggy took a closer look at the big pile of dirt. If he kind of scraped it together it would be about three feet high, and it would be a perfect ramp. He would bike down the sidewalk, up the ramp, and go flying through the air.

Cool!

Iggy scraped the dirt together so it was as

----

*You're not going to believe this, but the dirt and bark mixture is *another* gardening supply. It's called mulch, and guess what! It's usually got poop in it too! People spread it around their yards to make their plants grow better. Gardening is weird.

97

tall as it could be—maybe
even higher than three feet!—
and then he got back on his
bike and rode to the top of
the block.

He knew that the faster he rode, the farther he would fly through the air. But of course, he didn't want to fly *too* far because then he might fall off his bike. He decided on almost-but-not-quite top speed. Say, eight out of ten. Yeah, he thought, that would be good. Fast but not hyper-drive.

Okay.

He looked at the pile of dirt. He got on his bike. He started downhill.

GOOD RAMP

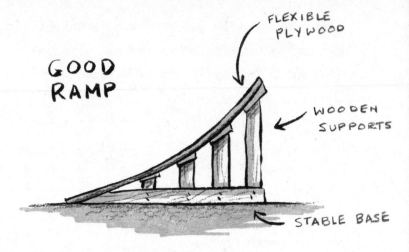

FLEXIBLE PLYWOOD

WOODEN SUPPORTS

STABLE BASE

QUESTIONABLE RAMP

PLYWOOD

CINDER BLOCK

TERRIBLE RAMP

MULCH

CHAPTER 14

GOOD NEWS, BAD NEWS

Here's some good news: The sidewalk sloped downward, but not a lot.

Here's some more good news: Iggy stuck to his plan and didn't go into hyperdrive. He stayed at eight out of ten.

That's all the good news.

Here's the bad news: Iggy wasn't thinking clearly about dirt. He wasn't thinking about the fact that ramps aren't usually made from dirt. They're usually made from wood or cement. Why? Because those things are hard. Dirt is soft. It is much, much softer than wood or cement. Even when you whomp it down, it's still pretty soft. So when you ride your bike into it, your bike sinks.

And when you are riding your bike fast and your bike sinks into dirt, your bike stops moving.

But guess what. *You* don't.

Iggy didn't.

Picture it in your mind: Iggy is riding down the sloping sidewalk, fast and faster. His bike reaches the big pile of dirt. The bike plows into the dirt and— *flump!*—comes to a stop. And what happens to Iggy?

He keeps going. He flies over the handlebars and through the air—

"YAAAAA

—and then he lands on his face.

Wait! Here is some more good news! Iggy didn't land on his face on the cement sidewalk.

He landed on his face on the grass between the sidewalk and the curb.

The grass was growing in dirt, of course. And what have we just learned about dirt?

It's soft!

Yay!

Because if Iggy had landed on his face on the cement sidewalk, his face probably would have been scraped off. Yuck.

But since he landed on the grass with dirt underneath it, his face was only a little bit scraped off.

That's good news, isn't it?

But there's bad news too: As Iggy was flying through the air, he was saying—okay, he was screeching— "YAAAAAAAAHH

Unfortunately, that meant his mouth was wide open when he hit the dirt. So the part of his face that was the most scraped-off was the inside of his mouth.

His nose was not too good either.

But his mouth was the worst. It was filled with sticks and dirt and grass and blood. For a minute, he just spat things out of his mouth. He hoped he wouldn't see a tooth. He was pretty sure he didn't see a tooth, but it was hard to tell, partly because his eyes were—well, let's just say they were watering—and partly because there was so much stuff in his mouth. He spat out a thing that was probably a rock. After he had spit all the stuff out of it, his mouth started to sting. And blood kept coming out of it too. And his nose hurt. And when he put his hand up to wipe his eyes, his hand came back with blood on it. *Ouch*. His mouth started to really, really sting.

The street was quiet and empty. There was nobody running toward him, saying, "Oh my gosh, Iggy! Are you okay?!"

He was all alone. He tried to say a bad word, but his mouth hurt too much.

He stood up—*ouch*—and limped, dripping and bleeding, back to the pile of dirt to get his bike. "Unless you're bleeding, don't bug me," his dad had said. It was time to go home.

CHAPTER 15

NOW THAT BLOOD IS POURING FROM HIS MOUTH, IGGY STOPS TO THINK

When he reached his house, Iggy stopped on the sidewalk. Sure, his mouth was bleeding and there was something wrong with his eyes—he hoped they weren't bleeding too—and every-thing was stinging and pounding. He could feel his heartbeat inside his nose, for instance.

But still, he didn't want to go inside.

Why? Because he knew that when he went inside, his dad was going to lose his mind.

His dad wasn't going to be mad, not with Iggy bleeding all over the place, but he was going to freak out. He was going to jump to his feet. He was going to yelp. There would be a lot of rushing around. There would be phone calls. His mom would get upset. She might even cry.

Standing there on the sidewalk, Iggy wished he wasn't about to walk into the house and ruin his dad's day. Which he had already ruined once by being suspended. He wished he hadn't been suspended. He wished he hadn't slammed Miss Hackerman in the shoulder with the basketball.

Was there something weird about him that he kept causing all this trouble? Maybe he was, actually, bad. Maybe BAD and IGGY *were* equal, and he just didn't know it. He knew for sure that if he hadn't done the thing with the gardening tape way back on Monday, he wouldn't have mashed his face today. Maybe mashing his face was a sign that he was supposed to be different. Better.

Better. Good. Quiet. Was he supposed to start being those things? Was he being taught a lesson?

Iggy sighed and walked toward the front door of his house.

HOW TO BE A BETTER PERSON, PART THREE

Well, I think you know what's going on here, kids! Iggy got what he deserved, didn't he? First he was bad, bad, bad, and then something terrible happened to him.

What have you learned today, kids?

You've learned that if you're bad, something terrible will happen to you.

So you must never, ever do anything bad (for instance, anything with gardening tape). If you do bad stuff, something terrible will happen to you (for instance, you will slam into the ground) and it will be all your fault.

You understand? If you're bad, you'll be sorry.

So don't be bad!

Got it?

Good.

Now that you have learned this important

lesson, you are on the highway to goodness!
What a great book this is! It's a shame it's almost over so you won't get much better than you are now.

CHAPTER 16

IGGY LEARNS HIS LESSON

The next day, Iggy went back to school with scabby, bloody scrapes on his face; one black eye that was really purple and green and one black eye that was really yellow; a giant Band-Aid over his nose, and a mouth full of stitches. Yup, that's right. Stitches on the *inside* of his mouth. Mostly on the inside of his bottom lip.

Did everyone look at Iggy and laugh? Did kids say, "You got what you deserved, Iggy Frangi, because you hit poor Miss Hackerman with a basketball." Did they say, "Ha! This happened because you're always so bad, Iggy!" Did Mrs. Wander come up to him and say, "I'm glad you hurt yourself, Iggy, because now you'll be a better person."

No.

Kids looked at him and said, "Eww! Gross!"

purple-and-green
black eye

scrape

yellow
black eye

Band-Aid

scrape

scrape

scrape

stitches

more
stitches

and "Dude! Wipeout!" and "Aaaaah!" and "I heard you got stitches in your mouth!" Then he would open his mouth, and they'd scream.

It was great.

I mean it. Sure, if a magic guy had shown up and said, "Iggy, would you like to go back in time and not mash your face up?" Iggy would have said yes. But since he couldn't go back in time, and his face *was* mashed up, it was fun to make people scream. It was fun to have the most mashed-up face in the school. It was fun to have everyone bunch around him, looking at his mouth and pretending to puke.

Ms. Schulberger winced when she saw him. "Oh, Iggy!" she said. "You poor kid!" Iggy smiled bravely (which actually did hurt), and Ms. Schulberger winced again. "If you need to lie down in the nurse's office, just let me know. Anytime, sweetie."

It was great.

At lunch, a fifth-grade kid who was famous for falling off the roof of the sports equipment shed came over to Iggy's table. He looked at Iggy's face and nodded. "Respect," he said.

It was great.

That afternoon in art, after they were done gluing their collages, six girls in Iggy's class—including Lainey!—made him Get Well Soon cards. Usually, Lainey ignored him.

It was great.

After school, as Iggy was leaving with Diego—who said he felt like throwing up every time he looked at Iggy—Mrs. Wander was standing by the gate. She called out, "Iggy Frangi!"

He froze.

Mrs. Wander stomped toward him, her eyeballs bulging.

What? What was she going to do to him?

"You fell off your bike," she said.

Iggy nodded.

She frowned. "I hope you'll learn to be more careful, Iggy."

Okay, that was not so great, but it could have been worse.

When he went home, he got ice cream for snack because he couldn't chew.

Great.

His dad brought him a Spider-Man book, because he felt bad about telling Iggy not to bug him.

Great.

As he lay in bed that night, Iggy touched his purple-and-green eye. It felt big, but it didn't hurt that much. The scabby parts of his face didn't hurt that much either. Even his nose didn't hurt a *lot*. The inside of his mouth, though—he poked it with his tongue—yow, that hurt.

But still, he thought, I'm not in trouble anymore. Nobody's mad at me.

Yeah, he thought. It was worth it.

CHAPTER 17

IGGY PLANTS FLOWERS BY THE SIDE OF THE ROAD

But the best part was yet to come. The best part happened two weeks later. It wasn't just the best part of that month or that year. It was one of the best things that ever happened to Iggy in his entire life.

Two weeks after Iggy mashed his face in the grass, he was mostly back to normal. Both of his black eyes were their regular color again. He only had one scab, on his forehead, and it was about to fall off. There was a yellow bruise and a tiny cut on his nose. Inside his mouth, all the stitches were gone, and he could chew stuff. There was one raised part on the inside of his cheek, but that was all.

Iggy felt pretty normal.

So, two weeks after wiping out, Iggy was sitting in Ms. Schulberger's classroom one afternoon, feeling normal. Ms. Schulberger was talking about What a Paragraph Is.

As far as Iggy could tell, it seemed like a paragraph could be anything. One sentence, two sentences, five hundred sentences.

Now Ms. Schulberger was talking about starting paragraphs with topic sentences. Iggy began to feel a little bit sleepy. He yawned. He still couldn't yawn all the way. He tried to balance his pencil on the tip of his finger.

"Iggy!" said Ms. Schulberger. "Listen up!"

Okay, okay. She talked more about topic sentences. Iggy poked around inside his mouth with his tongue. It was amazing that it didn't hurt anymore. It didn't hurt at all. It felt—wait. What was that? He ran his tongue over the inside of his lower lip. There was a lump in it. A long, thin lump.

What was it?

He couldn't figure it out.

He raised his hand.

"Yes, Iggy?" said Ms. Schulberger.

"Can I go to the bathroom?" He bugged his eyes out so she would know he really had to go.

She nodded. "Scoot."

Iggy scooted. He scooted out the door, down the hallway, and into the bathroom, where he leaned close to the mirror and pulled his lower lip down to take a look.

And he could not believe what he saw there.

THERE WAS A BLADE OF GRASS GROWING INSIDE HIS MOUTH.

It was growing under his skin, but he could still see it. A tiny piece of it was poking out of his skin, and it was green. The rest of it was in a line right where his stitches had been. It was growing sideways. It looked like it was smiling at him.

It was the coolest thing he'd ever seen.

He ran back to class. "Ms. Schulberger!" he yelled from the doorway. "Look!"

Ms. Schulberger didn't like it when he yelled. "Iggy! I've told you—"

"No! Really! Check this out!" Iggy came to stand in front of her. "Look!" He pulled down his lip. "It's grass!"

She looked. And then she jumped back. "Oh my gosh!" she said. "It *is* grass!"

All the kids came rushing up to look. And then they screamed. "OOOOOH!" "IT'S GRASS!" "GRO-OSSS!"

Iggy turned to Ms. Schulberger. "Please, please, please take a picture, Ms. Schulberger. Please!"

Ms. Schulberger was shaking her head with amazement. "There's *grass* growing in your mouth, Iggy," she said. "You're a biome!" She got her phone and took a picture.

Iggy nodded. He was a biome. A seed must have been sewed into his skin when they did the stitches, and now he was growing grass in his mouth. He poked at it with his tongue.

Ms. Schulberger told him he could go to the nurse's office to have it taken out. "No way," said Iggy. "I'm going to leave it in there until it grows out of my mouth."

But once he sat back at his desk and Ms. Schulberger was talking about topic sentences again, he couldn't help poking at it. Then he couldn't help very, very gently biting the tiny

green piece between his teeth and his tongue, and very, very gently pulling.

Ms. Schulberger kept talking about topic sentences, but she also kept looking at Iggy. Pretty soon everyone else in class was looking at Iggy too.

Iggy was the only one who could concentrate, and he was concentrating very hard on pulling the blade of grass out of his skin, a little bit at a time.

He didn't want to break it.

Ms. Schulberger stopped talking to watch.

All the kid turned around in their desks to watch.

Iggy worked on the inside of his mouth.

He almost had it.

Almost.

Almost.

Then, with a squeak only he could hear, Iggy pulled the blade of grass out of his mouth.

"Did it!" he shouted, and held it up for everyone to see.

"Ew-wwww!" shrieked the class.

Arch started to stomp. "Igg-Y! Igg-Y!" he yelled. Owen stomped too, and so did Donal and Nhat and Aidan.

Ms. Schulberger began to laugh. She dropped into her chair and laughed and laughed and laughed. "I love my job," she gasped.

Aidan waved a dollar. "I'll buy it off you!"

"No way," said Iggy, holding his grass tight. "I'm going to keep it. Forever."

And he did.

He taped the blade of grass in a special book, and under it, he wrote, "The best thing that ever happened to me!!!"

Which it was, until about four and a half months later.

But that's a different story.

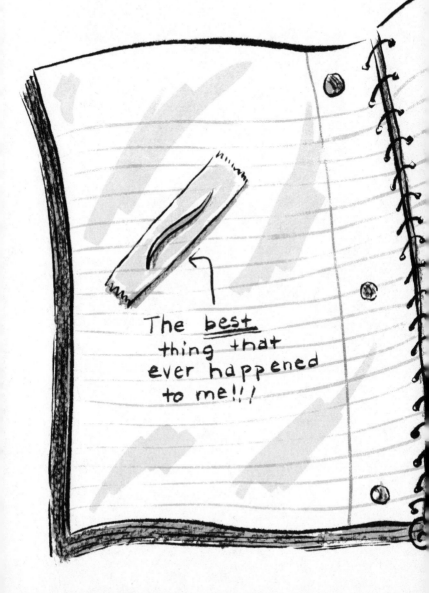

The **best** thing that ever happened to me!!!

CHAPTER 18

BETTER NOT

Bummer. Iggy's not any better than he was at the beginning of this book. He did one bad thing and then another (although we all can agree that he did the second thing by mistake), and then he got his face mashed up. It seemed like he was about to learn to be a better person. But then he didn't.

It's okay with him. In the end, Iggy decided that he is fine the way he is.

I think so too.

But you?

All I can say is: I hope you've learned your lesson.

photo credit: Amy Perl Photography

ANNIE BARROWS doesn't want to ruin this book by telling you what happens in it. But she really, really wants to say that the thing in this book you will find the most unbelievable—it involves something green—that thing is TRUE! It actually happened to a guy she knows at the gym. And guess what. He still has it, the green thing, in a scrapbook. How disgusting!

anniebarrows.com

@anniebarrowsauthor

SAM RICKS is the illustrator of the Geisel Award winner *Don't Throw It to Mo!* and the Stinkbomb and Ketchup-Face books. He is grateful his parents let him live through a surprising number of Iggycidents.

Sam lives with his family in Utah.

samricks.com

@samuelricks

DON'T MISS IGGY'S NEXT TRIUMPHS

IGGY
IS THE
HERO OF EVERYTHING